scarred perfection

Khloe Wren

ISBN: 978-1-922942-06-7
Copyright © Khloe Wren 2023

Cover Credits:
Images: Deposit Photos
Digital Artist: Khloe Wren
Editing Credits:
Editor: Carolyn Depew of Write Right
Proofreader: Kelly Klau

author note

This story takes place in Outback South Australia (see map below), so I've written it in my native language: Australian English. This is similar to British English but with some bonuses! It's a little different to US English. I've included a glossary of the Aussie stuff to help out.

glossary

Things

- Bench: A counter.
- Bloke: Man.
- Eureka: Aussie slang term of excitement used when someone discovers something they were looking for. It became known as what gold miners would call out when they discovered gold during the Australian Gold Rush.
- Oi: A greeting similar to "hey".
- Roadhouse: In the outback, a roadhouse often doubles as the only store in town. They have petrol/gas pumps out the front, and inside the store they have grocery items as well as the normal

petrol station items and snack foods. Sometimes they also include a bar and sell alcohol.

- Road train: A conventional prime mover truck pulling two or more trailers. Commonly used to transport goods between States in Australia.
- Spanner: A tool used to loosen or tighten nuts. Called a wrench in the US.
- Ute: A vehicle with a tray on the back, and either a single or dual cab on the front. Called a "truck" in the US.

Places

- Walawuru: Fictional town located roughly where Lyndhurst is in South Australia.
- Adelaide: Capital city of South Australia.

one

Standing up straight, Kane stretched out his spine. Something wasn't right. His whole body was on edge, like he was about to enter a fight. Rolling his shoulders, he turned and dropped his spanner into his toolbox before glancing at his twin. Jeremy stood, rubbing his palm over the back of his neck as he looked over to the roadhouse on the other side of the highway.

"You feel it too?"

"Yeah, something bad has happened. C'mon, let's go check it out."

His stomach was in knots as he rushed out of the garage. Jeremy flipped over their "Back in five" sign while Kane yanked down the roller door on their auto repair shop. A quick glance up and down the outback highway showed it was all clear, so he and his twin jogged across toward the old homestead that had been converted into the town's only roadhouse and store. By the time he had his palm on the store's front door, his heart was pounding, and his instincts were screaming. Whatever was going on, it was big.

The door let out a little squeak and the alarm dinged loudly, echoing around the interior. Which, while it wasn't unusual for there to be no customers, it was strange for the counter to be unmanned. Normally Paul, Carol, or their daughter, Abigail, would be in here. If whoever was working had nipped out the back, they'd have come out when the door alarm sounded.

He turned to face his twin. "Can you remember if Abigail was due home this weekend?"

"Not sure. She hasn't been home in a few weeks, so it's possible."

Abigail was twenty years old and taking an accounting course two hundred miles away in Port Augusta. While it was considerably closer than where she'd been living for high school, it was still far enough away that she didn't come home all that regularly. Kane would never forget when she'd first headed off to Adelaide for boarding school.

He and Jeremy had only recently

discovered that Abigail was destined to be their mate, so when she left, they'd both felt hollow and empty. Not being able to see her every day and know she was safe and well had been hell on Kane's nerves. Unfortunately, with them being two years older than her, they had both already left school to begin their apprenticeships. There'd been no way for them to leave Walawuru and follow her.

When she finished school last year, he'd hoped she would move back home, but nope. She'd moved on with her education. Both he and Jeremy were so damn proud of her for being smart enough to go as far as she had with her schooling—they simply wished it didn't take her so far away from them.

When she did make the journey home, both he and his twin tried to see her as much as possible, but that was tricky. There were rules in place by which they had to abide, and he didn't mean human laws. Kane and Jeremy were Wedge-tailed eagle shifters and their clan here in Walawuru had their own set of rules all members must obey. The ones that had caused them the most stress were the ones regarding claiming a mate.

Male shifters began changing forms during puberty when their hormones began surging.

On the other hand, females didn't shift until after they'd bonded with their male, or males. In order to prevent females rushing into bonding while they were young simply so they could begin shifting, the elders had decreed that females were not to be told about the existence of shapeshifters until they were twenty-one years old. It was also their law that females couldn't bond before that age.

Like human males, male shifters also started paying more attention to the opposite sex after puberty. He and Jeremy had both been drawn to Abigail from the moment their hormones kicked in and they realized what girls were all about. They'd been lucky to find their mate so early in life, even if it had meant they needed to stand by and wait for her to come of age. That wasn't the only thing he and his twin had to worry about. Sweet Abigail had been adopted by fully human parents. Kane had no idea how Paul and Carol were going to react to their daughter being claimed by two men when she was finally old enough.

With his heart in his throat, he followed Jeremy around the counter toward the back room. The moment he stepped into that small office, his mouth went dry, and his palms began to sweat. Paul and Carol were intently watching a small screen where a grainy image of an SUV taking off from their driveway had Carol sobbing.

"Is everything all right?"

At the sound of Jeremy's voice, Carol gasped and spun to face them.

"Sorry, Carol, I didn't mean to scare you. When no one came out to the shop, we got worried and thought we'd check if you were all okay."

"They took her! Those bastards stole my baby!"

A wave of dizziness passed through Kane as his blood drained from his head. He threw out a hand, catching the edge of a shelf to steady himself. He'd been hopeful the bad feeling they'd felt was due to her injuring herself or something like that. Not that she'd been abducted. But Kane knew full well that there was only one person Carol would refer to as her baby. Abigail may be twenty years old, but she would always be her adoptive mother's baby girl.

Jeremy bumped his shoulder into Kane's, jarring him out of his daze. His twin guided him forward a couple of steps until they could see the screen more clearly. The moment his gaze focused on the image of the front of the shop where the petrol pumps were, his mind cleared. He needed to gather as much information as he could, then he and Jeremy would go rescue their mate.

"I'll rewind it for you. Did you see something from your place? Is that why you came over?"

Kane tried to keep his expression neutral at Paul's hopeful tone. He and Jeremy had both been working under a car this morning. Neither would have been able to see a thing. He wasn't admitting that to Carol yet. He wanted to see what the video would reveal. Just because they hadn't bonded with her didn't mean Abigail wasn't theirs. They would protect their mate with everything they had.

A mix of fear and fury had Kane's stomach in knots when Paul reached to set the player going. He held his breath for a few moments when the silent feed showed a dark-coloured early nineties model Nissan Patrol pull up at the southernmost pump. A slender man began filling the vehicle with fuel while a stockier bloke headed for the shop. Kane frowned at the screen when, a moment later, the same man came out the door. That was a little odd.

"He asked me where the toilet was."

Carol's words were whispered in a harsh,

pain-filled voice that had him wincing. Without taking his eyes from the screen, Kane instinctively raised a hand to lightly grip her shoulder for a few seconds, attempting to give her some comfort.

The bigger bloke walked out of the camera's field as the slender one finished pumping petrol and headed inside the shop. Kane's heart beat double time when action exploded on the screen. The man returned from the direction of the toilets with his arms full of pissed off female. Abigail was kicking and pulling at the hand over her mouth, but the man didn't give her a chance to escape his grip. The back door of the Nissan opened, and he passed her to someone before he jumped in behind her. Kane clenched his fists at his sides as his body vibrated with rage. He barely noticed when the third man strolled from the shop, got in the car, and they drove off heading north.

"Fuck me. That's at least three men with her. We need to find her fast."

Red filled Kane's vision then it shifted to infrared. His fury and overwhelming need to protect his mate had brought forward his animal side. If he wasn't careful, he'd fully shift to his eagle form, which he couldn't allow to happen at the moment. Squeezing his eyes shut, he took several deep breaths. He had to calm down and get his human vision back. He didn't have the best depth perception when his eagle sight kicked in while he was still in human form. Somehow, he doubted Paul and Carol would be impressed if he started bumping into everything while he attempted to leave the room. They certainly wouldn't believe he was capable of saving their only daughter if he couldn't even navigate his way out of an office. Taking another deep breath, he opened his eyes and blinked several times. Relief had him exhaling in a rush. His body had calmed and was now fully human, however his mind was still whirling. If only he and Jeremy had bonded with her, she would have had one of them with her today. She'd also have been able to shift to her eagle form to fly away from anyone wanting to hurt her.

He turned to Jeremy as he rubbed his aching chest. "Call the elders. They can start things here while we go north searching. I don't want to waste time preparing."

Kane knew Jeremy understood where he was coming from. He couldn't sit there poring over maps when he could be out there looking.

Their head elder, Nathan, could telepathically guide them if they discovered anything.

Paul sighing heavily behind him had Kane turning his attention toward the man with a frown. He hadn't thought Paul and Carol knew about their kind.

"I've already called Nathan. I'd just hung up when you two came through the door. He's notifying the other elders before he comes in."

Kane wasn't sure how much they knew, so he needed to be careful about what, if anything, he disclosed to them. Non-shifters weren't meant to even know of their existence, let alone any specific details like the name of their head elder. Although, Paul and Carol were in a different category due to adopting a child who was a shifter. Kane supposed eventually they would have to learn everything about the shifter world. They would need to be given a damn good reason before they'd be okay with their daughter entering into a permanent ménage. Regardless of all the reasons, it wasn't his or Jeremy's place to educate them. The elders needed to do that. Kane rubbed his eyes. Maybe it would be easier to just drop the subject altogether for now and get moving on finding their mate.

"Jeremy and I vow to you that we will not stop until we find her and bring her back."

After Paul gave them a firm nod, Kane followed his twin out of the room. Determination to rescue Abigail focused his mind as he followed Jeremy from the roadhouse. The time stamp on the video was only fifteen minutes ago, but they were on the open highway with a full tank of fuel. Unless they could find a thermal to help them build extra speed, it could take hours to catch up. And that was only if Abigail's kidnappers stayed on the highway, which Kane's instincts told him they weren't going to do for long. A heaviness settled in his stomach as more doubts crept into his mind.

"Let me lock up the shop, then we'll head off. We will find her, Kane."

Jeremy knew Kane better than anyone else. His twin knew the thoughts he was currently fighting against, because he was having the same damn thoughts.

"I know we will. It's how long it's going to take us that has me worried. That and what those bastards will do to our sweet Abigail before we can get to her."

All shifters were unnaturally beautiful, but their Abigail was perfection. Her hair was a chocolate brown with dark red streaks through it. It always looked soft. Kane had dreamed many times about running his fingers through those tresses as he kissed her lush lips. Her skin was pale and smooth, not even a freckle marring her flesh. Her curves were subtle and graceful. Her small breasts would fill his palms perfectly. She was quite simply everything he'd ever wanted in a woman.

Kane knew neither he nor Jeremy would stop until she was found, no matter how long it took. But he was praying they found her quickly. The thought of her being harmed nearly brought him to his knees.

He took a deep breath and released it with a sigh. They needed to be smart about this. It was most likely going to take a serious amount of time to find her, and wearing them both out in the first hours wasn't going to help anyone, least of all Abigail. They would both also lose their minds when Nathan forced them to rest if they did push too hard, which they would in a heartbeat to find their mate.

"With the head start they have, Jer, we might be better off to go out one at a time. That way we can look for her nonstop till we find her."

His twin nodded. "Good idea. You take

first shift in the sky. I'll get in contact with Nathan and coordinate things from here until we switch over."

Tears stung Abigail's eyes as she thrashed against the man holding her. Damn it, she wouldn't be snatched from her home like this! Panic rose within her the longer she struggled to no avail. The man behind her had her wrapped up tightly in a bear hug from which she just couldn't break free. She opened her mouth to scream, but her attacker quickly slammed his hand over her lips.

"Stay silent or I'll break your fucking jaw."

She rolled her shoulders, determined to loosen his hold now he only had one arm around her body, but he was so much bigger than her, she still couldn't get free. Giving up on trying to get out of his grip, she focused on her unbound legs. Lifting her right knee up as far as she could, she then put all her energy into kicking her foot back as fast and hard as she could. Her heel connected with solid muscle, but all he did was grunt and tighten the arm around her torso. She growled out her frustration as he dragged her from where she'd been cleaning the bathrooms around the side of her parents' small roadhouse. She refused to give in and be taken without a fight. She made no effort to walk, forcing him to take all her weight, and she kept up with the kicking and twisting her upper body the entire way. Every time she landed a hit, a spark of hope would flare, but he never loosened his hold or slowed his stride enough for her to break free.

When they cleared the side of the roadhouse, she frantically looked around for someone. Anyone. Despite being in the middle of the outback, her parents' place was the last chance for hundreds of miles for people to get petrol, so they often had customers. Her body started shaking and her heart sank when she saw there was only one vehicle, and they were moving toward it. Where were her parents? She threw her weight to the side, forcing her kidnapper to turn slightly, enough for her to see the door, which was closed tight. The windows were covered by blinds. Her throat tightened and she struggled to get enough air through her nose.

With a curse, he pulled her back toward the dark blue SUV. Her body was getting tired, but when the rear door opened and another man, after pausing a moment, reached out for her, adrenaline gave her a second wind. Her body continued to tremble, but she ignored it and put every ounce of energy she could muster into fighting the firm grip she was in. This couldn't be happening! Tears clouded her vision.

"Take her already, before she busts my damn knee."

A small flicker of pride ran through her that she'd managed to at least hurt the bastard who'd grabbed her. Waiting for any opportunity to flee, she held herself tense, but his hold on her didn't lessen until the other man had a firm grip on her. She was being hauled into the back of the vehicle before she could even yell out for help.

In the chaos of everyone getting into the SUV, she continued to fight the men until pain and heat flared across the side of her face and her head snapped to the side as her initial captor backhanded her. As she panted through the shock and pain, her wrists were grabbed and cuffed. When they lifted her hands, she pulled hard to keep them down, but it did no good. They attached them to a hook in the roof as though she weren't fighting back at all.

By the time her original kidnapper took hold of her ankles and cuffed them to a thick chain anchored to the floor, she had nothing left to fight. Closing her eyes, she mustered all her remaining energy and pulled on all her limbs, testing her bonds, but none of them gave at all. She let her head drop forward against her chest for a moment as a wave of dizziness hit her. She was well and truly caught. When the rear door slammed, it jolted her out of her misery and got her thinking again.

Her parents' roadhouse wasn't a new building. Unlike the ones nearer the city, it didn't have a glass front where anyone inside could see everything that happened outside. It was an old stone homestead that had been converted to fit their needs. There were only two windows and a screen door on the wall facing her, but she'd already seen that the blinds were drawn over the windows, which was normal on a hot day. As was the fact the solid timber door had been shut. When she'd been younger, her parents were forever telling her to close doors to keep in the cool, air-conditioned air. Tears pricked her eyes as she thought about her parents. Would she ever see them again? They'd feel so guilty for not noticing when she'd been taken.

Confirming all her thoughts, a man came out the screen door, pulling the solid one shut as he moved. There hadn't been more than a split second where someone would have been able to see out, and even if her father or mother had been looking in that direction, they wouldn't have noticed her through the vehicle's tinted windows. She wanted to scream and shout, to thrash around until she was free, but deep down she knew it would only serve to get her hit again. And still, no one would have seen her being taken. Suddenly, a little kernel of hope sparked. The Gibson twins. Maybe they'd been looking over at the road from their workshop. If they'd seen her being hauled away, she was certain they'd come to her rescue.

A flash of heat passed through her as she thought of Kane and Jeremy Gibson. The twins had featured in all her fantasies. They were tall and lean, with broad shoulders and muscular bodies—built like men should be. When she was home visiting, she often gazed over toward their garage, hopeful she'd be able to catch a glimpse of them.

As the driver's door was opened, she shook her head. She didn't have time to waste on memories. A few butterflies fluttered in her stomach as she twisted her neck to look over her shoulder, hoping she would see them running to her rescue. The butterflies turned to stone. No one was there. Not a single person was anywhere.

A chill ran up her spine and she tried to swallow past the lump in her throat when the car started. She caught the driver's gaze in the rearview mirror, but aside from his eyes widening for a moment, he showed no reaction to discovering a cuffed woman in his vehicle. Clenching her hands into fists, she pushed down the unwanted tears that pricked her eyes. Anger rose as she struggled to compose herself. She wasn't some wilting flower that was going to meekly go to the slaughter. Damn, she hoped they didn't plan to murder her. Allowing her fury to grow, she turned and glared at the man closest to her.

"You won't get away with this. Any minute now, it'll be discovered I'm missing, then you'll have half the town on your heels until you release me."

She had no experience with trying to negotiate with kidnappers, but she had to at least try. With no chance of breaking free physically, talking her way out was the only option she had left.

"I don't think so, doll. No one saw us take you, and it looked to me like you'd only just started cleaning. I reckon we have at least a half hour before anyone even notices you're missing, let alone goes looking for you."

Abigail clenched her jaw. She knew he was right, but she sure as hell wasn't going to give him the satisfaction of agreeing out loud with the bastard. Once the vehicle cleared the town, they sped up. Slumping back, her head rested against the cool glass behind her as the bush and desert rushed past the windows in front of her. Accepting there was nothing she could do to escape until they stopped somewhere, she let her muscles relax. She hoped when they did stop, she would have enough energy to make another attempt at freedom. With her mind no longer focused on escaping, it whirled with other questions.

"Why'd you take me?"

She was almost too scared to ask, but knowledge was power, and maybe if she knew why they'd taken her, she would have better luck talking them into letting her go. And maybe if she had some time to mentally prepare herself, whatever they had planned wouldn't be so bad.

"Information."

She frowned and turned her face to stare at the one who'd spoken. She'd expected them to say something more physical. What could she possibly know that they wanted?

"I can't think of anything I know that would be important. Well, not unless you need an accountant, that is."

With deep scowls on their faces, the two men turned from her to look at each other.

"Are you sure she's one of them?"

"She's too pretty to be human, and you know it. And look at her damn hair! Those red streaks don't come naturally, and I'm fairly certain there's no hairdressers this far out that would get that fancy."

Not human? Her stomach churned and that chill ran up her spine again. These men were insane or on drugs, and if they truly believed she knew something she didn't, this was going to get messy and painful for her.

"She obviously can't shift at will yet, or she'd have flown the coop when you snatched her."

She sat up straight. A wave of heat flowed over her as anger overtook her fear. Nothing set her temper off quite like being spoken about as though she weren't in the room. And nothing pushed her fear aside quite like losing her temper did.

"What the bloody hell are you two on about?"

"Wedge-tailed eagle shapeshifters are what we're on about, doll. We know they're real, and that you're one of them, so don't try to deny it."

Abigail shook her head as her mind spun. "I'm sorry, you think *what* is real?"

"Shapeshifters. People who can change from human into an animal, in your case, a Wedge-tailed eagle."

She squeezed her eyes shut on a silent prayer for help. She'd been kidnapped by lunatics.

A loud crack filled the air at the same time her head whipped back, smacking hard against the glass behind her. Pain ricocheted around her skull, and her sight grew fuzzy for a few moments.

"Don't ignore us, doll. You will answer our questions. Every single one of them."

With the side of her face still throbbing, she glared at them as her body tensed with her rage. "I can't tell you what I don't know, and this is the first I've ever heard of shapeshifters of any kind being real."

She winced and tensed in readiness for another blow when the face of the man who'd snatched her turned red and his eyes filled with rage. Whatever he was about to do was going to seriously hurt.

"Stop lying, bitch!"

Seeing his fist coming at her face, she tried to twist away from the impact, but her bound hands and feet wouldn't allow it. She gasped for breath as agony exploded through her head before everything went dark.

two

Jeremy took a deep breath and tried to dispel the dread that had his hands and arms trembling. Unable to type, he pushed his chair back from the desk and rubbed his face with his palms. His and Kane's mate had been kidnapped. Snatched from under their noses in broad daylight. The knowledge that Kane was currently out flying the skies trying to find any sign of Abigail or the dark Nissan that had taken her away from them was the only thing that was keeping him somewhat level-headed. But he wouldn't be able to relax until they had her back.

As edgy as Jeremy felt, he knew Kane had been even more so. Of the two of them, Jeremy had always been the more even tempered one, while Kane was quick to anger or jump into a fight. It had seemed like the right thing to do to offer to take the first shift at their garage while Kane flew.

With a sigh, he got up and went over to the fridge to grab a bottle of water. The cold liquid relieved his dry mouth and throat. After a few swallows, he headed back to the desk. Holding his hands out, he smiled when they didn't shake. He could get back to work now.

Despite not being out there physically searching for Abigail, he wasn't sitting on his hands or twiddling his thumbs while he waited for his turn to fly. He had every map they owned spread out over the desk and floor, along with his computer loaded up with a satellite image of the area. The national shifter council had some neat toys they were more than happy to share with anyone who needed them to keep their clans safe. He was compiling a list of places that could be used to hold someone.

"Jer, you there?"

"Yeah, Kane. I'm here. Any sight of them?"

"Nothing. All I've seen are a few road trains. How's that list going? Because following the road is useless. It's been hours, and I haven't seen any sign of them. They had to have turned off somewhere."

A glance at the clock told Jeremy it had

been two hours since Abigail was taken. If they'd stuck with the main highway, Kane would have at least seen them by now. He'd have flown high enough to see further into the distance. He swallowed past the lump in his throat. He knew Kane was right. Hell, he'd just been thinking the same thing. They'd turned off somewhere and were hiding while they did heaven knew what to their mate.

"Give me a minute. I've listed every ruin in the area. I'm just checking with the satellite to find ones that are actually capable of being used by them."

Now that he'd finished listing all of the buildings in disrepair near the road north from Walawuru, he was using the real time satellite images to find each one to look for signs of life. Most were barely more than a pile of rubble surrounding an old fire stack, so those he could quickly discount. Places like Farina, where the entire town was in ruins, were too popular with tourists to be an option.

The longer it took, the tighter his chest felt, but he didn't slow. He had to find the information his twin needed. No matter how focused he was on searching, his mind couldn't stop thinking about what her captors could have done to her in two hours. How much had she already suffered? How long would it take to find where they were holding her?

Forcing his hands to move, he typed in the next lot of coordinates and hit enter. After zooming in on an old stone homestead, he sat straighter when he saw most of its walls were still standing along with a few sheets of iron on one end of the building. This had possibilities, despite the fact he couldn't see any vehicles or tire tracks around it. He leaned in closer to the screen as he zoomed in further and rubbed his eyes to make sure he wasn't imagining what he saw. A glint of sunlight off metal. Rolling the mouse wheel again, the screen blurred then cleared as it focused in closer on the small white dot until he could work out what it was.

"Eureka!"

Hope loosened the pressure in his chest as he'd finally discovered a promising lead. A vehicle under camo mesh, the corner of the front bumper poking through and reflecting the sun's rays. Scrolling over to the homestead, he followed the outside walls and discovered a section of the house also covered with another mesh tarp. Between that and the section with iron on the roof, it was more than large enough to hide Abigail and her three captors.

"What have you found, Jeremy?"

Nathan, their clan's head elder, had flown over as soon as he heard of Abigail's abduction. He'd initially stayed with Abigail's parents but had later joined Jeremy to help put the list together. Jeremy had no idea how old Nathan was, but he'd told the younger generation many times that he was old enough that he didn't want to know anything about computers.

"A car and house covered with camo mesh. It's the most promising thing I've found so far. I'll keep looking, but this is definitely worth checking out."

"Can you explain to Kane how to find it, or would you prefer I speak with him so you can keep searching?"

Normally, shifters could only telepathically communicate with their immediate family and their mates. Due to him being the head elder, Nathan could speak with the entire clan. Like all skills, the more a shifter practiced, the better he became. Since Jeremy and Kane had been chatting mind-to-mind since before they could crawl, their bond was solid, and they could use it over vast distances without an issue.

Theoretically, they could speak to Abigail, too. She was theirs. But for some reason, neither he nor Kane could get through to her.

Whenever a shifter successfully connected to another telepathically, he felt a slight buzz through his mind. They'd both tried a few times over the past hours to enter her mind, but they hadn't been able to even make a connection.

"I'll send him an image of the map, then keep searching. I'll be quick."

Jeremy took a deep breath, closed his eyes, and pushed the image of the map into his twin's mind.

"That far out? You sure?"

"I caught a glint of metal under some camo mesh. It's suspicious enough to warrant checking out."

"This is the only lead you've found?"

"Yeah, nothing else fits. This is the first ruin I've found with a vehicle nearby, and they've tried to hide themselves from anything above."

"You thinking what I am? Could these be some crazies after a shifter?"

"I was just wondering precisely that. Abigail doesn't hide her natural hair colour, and she's beyond beautiful. This could be an attack on the clan rather than a random snatch and grab."

Jeremy rubbed his aching chest. Every so often, their clan had trouble with a group of idiots that called themselves "scientists" wanting to capture a shifter to prove they existed. So far, they hadn't succeeded. Everyone in the clan knew exactly who the crazies were, and no way would any shifter insult actual scientists by calling them anything other than crazy. But if this was them, they could have done any number of horrific things to their precious mate trying to get her to shift forms for them.

"It'll take me at least fifteen minutes to get to that location. Hopefully, I can catch a thermal and get there faster, but I'm running on empty after being in the air for so long. If this one turns up vacant, I'll head back, and we'll switch. My wings need a break."

"Sounds good. Let me know when you get there."

Cutting off communication with his twin, he turned to face Nathan. "What's your gut telling you? Are these shifter crazies, or a random attack?"

The way the older man sighed heavily had a cold shiver pass through him.

"I fear this is an attempt on our clan. Have you or Kane been able to reach her?"

He shook his head. "We've both been trying since she was taken, but we can't even make a connection. Do you know any reason why we wouldn't be able to connect with her?"

He silently prayed Nathan's response wasn't going to confirm his worst fear. That they weren't truly mates. That he and his twin had been wrong all these years.

"Sometimes metal affects shifters, especially young females who haven't trained their minds to accept the connection. My first guesses would be that she's being restrained with chains or metal cuffs, being held in a barred cage, or it could be that she's unconscious."

His gut twisted and a bad taste filled his mouth. "So you don't think it's because we're not mates?"

Nathan gave him a look that indicated the older man thought he'd lost his mind.

"Jeremy, you and Kane are clearly Abigail's destined males. Besides, I can't reach her either."

Jeremy stretched his neck to each side, trying to relieve some of his tension. He really didn't like the idea of his mate being restrained in any way, let alone being at the mercy of the crazies.

"Kane mentioned he was going to come in after he checks out this place to switch with me. I might as well head out and meet him there."

He couldn't sit still any longer, and his instincts were flaring like never before that they were close to her, and she was in trouble. If she wasn't at the site he'd found, Kane would be back here to continue looking for other locations while he stayed out searching.

Abigail woke to an insistent pounding inside her skull. With a groan, she went to rub her aching temples and jaw, but she stilled when she couldn't move her arms at all.

"Finally, she's awake. I'm going to get my stuff so we can get started."

Her heart rate tripled. Being kidnapped hadn't simply been a bad dream, it was reality. Licking her dry lips, she opened her eyes and quickly slammed them shut again as agony drilled into her skull. After taking a deep breath, she tried again, this time slowly opening her lids while bracing for the shock of the bright, harsh light aimed at her. Needing to evaluate exactly how stuffed she was, she blinked a few times to clear her vision. Once her eyesight cleared enough that she could scan her surroundings, she winced. There wasn't much to see. Swallowing past the lump in her throat, she took in the crumbling stone walls around her and the roof that was comprised of a mix of sheets of rusty iron and a weird-looking netting thing made out of fabric in different shades of green.

While it was clear she was in one of the old ruins that dotted the outback landscape, she had no clue which one, not that it mattered. She needed to get free of her captors before she could go anywhere. With another deep breath, she switched her focus to assess how stuck she was. She was firmly tied to a sturdy wooden chair with rough rope that was digging into her wrists and ankles harshly as she strained to break free.

Tears pricked her eyes, but she refused to let them fall. Despite the fact she was in a whole heap of trouble with no obvious way out, she refused to let these whack jobs see her as some weak, crying female. While she battled against her rising panic, she let her head fall forward, hiding her face with her hair. She'd been snatched from her home, and her kidnappers wanted her to give them information she wasn't sure even existed. No way was this day going to end well for her. An image of her parents filled her mind. Would she ever see them again?

The sound of water had her twisting her head to face a tall, slender man she recognized as the driver, pouring water from a large bottle into a cup. She tried to swallow, but her parched throat wouldn't cooperate past screaming at her for the relief she could see. Was it worth the risk of asking for some? She didn't want them to start hitting her again.

The man strolled up to her and pressed the cup to her lower lip. Clenching her jaw, she glanced back toward the bottle. What if it wasn't water? Would they poison her?

"It's just water. You saw me open the bottle and pour it."

She hadn't seen him open the bottle. She couldn't trust him.

The man sighed then lifted the cup to his own mouth, taking a swallow. "There. Happy?"

She frowned up at him. Why was he being nice? The cup was once more pressed against her lower lip, and this time she opened her mouth. He tilted it up and she closed her eyes as the cool liquid soothed her throat. She drank as fast as she could until she'd polished off the entire thing. She didn't want to risk him getting sick of holding the cup and take it away before she got as much as she could. With no idea when she'd get another drink, she had to make the most of every opportunity to up her chances of survival.

"Thank you."

He nodded slightly at her whispered words.

"What are you doing? She's not some pampered pet! We certainly don't need to be wasting water on her. Or time. We won't have long before they find us. No matter what we do, they always find us if we don't get done within a couple of hours."

"I just figured out here in this heat, she'll dehydrate in no time, then she'll die before she tells us anything. Fat lot of good that'll do any of us."

She winced at his words. So much for the vague hope one of her captors actually had some common decency. The man who'd snatched her just grunted and set a large toolbox on the table near her. She began trembling as fear coursed through her while she tried once more to break free of the ropes that were keeping her restrained, but they still held strong.

"I swear I don't know anything! I have no idea what you're even talking about."

The slender man gave her a pitying look but stayed silent. Again, tears threatened, but she forced them down. She would not let these bastards see her cry.

"Abigail? Can you hear me?"

Stilling, she held her breath as she once more glanced around the room, frowning. Who'd spoken to her? The voice was familiar, like she'd heard it before, but it sounded echoey, as if it were inside her head. What the hell was wrong with her?

"Don't speak aloud. Do what you do when you talk to yourself, and I'll hear it."

She released her breath slowly and caught sight of the man laying out all sorts of nasty-looking tools on the table. What did she have to lose? Even if her mind had cracked and a figment of her imagination was talking to her, it was better than suffering through what was about to happen alone.

"Who are you?"

"My name is Nathan Reid. You've met me in your parents' shop many times."

No wonder his voice seemed familiar. She had indeed met him many times. Her heart lightened a little as she pictured the older man in her mind. Every time he saw her, he'd ask how her schooling was going. He'd always been kind to her.

"Why are you in my head?"

"Because you are one of us, and I am the clan elder."

Her mind spun and she closed her eyes while allowing her head to hang forward once more. She hoped it would keep her expression hidden from her captors, because there was no way she could hide her shock as terror seeped through her.

"One of you? So these crackpots are for real?"

"Well, that depends on what they told you. If they told you that you are a Wedged-tailed eagle shapeshifter and not fully human, then yes, they told you the truth."

"That's a little hard to believe, since I've never been able to change into a bird."

She winced as she tried to convince herself she was really having this conversation. Maybe she had, in fact, gone mad.

"Female shifters can't change form until after they bond with their mate, or in your case, mates."

"Sorry, what?"

She wasn't sure how to even begin to process any of that statement.

"You know Kane and Jeremy Gibson... how you feel drawn to them? That's because they are your destined males. Our society has rules. Rules that say females can't be approached by their males until after they've turned twenty-one. They've been waiting for you for years now."

"That's why they hover but never get too close?"

She'd wondered what they'd been playing at all these years. Many times their rejection of her had kept her away. She missed her parents but didn't visit as often as she could because it hurt too much to watch them avoid her.

"They are searching for you. I promise, neither will rest until you are rescued."

"How do they know where I am? I don't even know!"

"Trust in fate, Abigail. They'll find you. I believe Jeremy has located you on his fancy computer and is on his way to meet Kane there."

She winced and leaned away when she heard heavy footfalls on the dirt floor beside her. She slowly raised her head to see he'd finished arranging his tools and was now standing beside her chair with an evil grin on his face and a large, very sharp-looking hunting knife in his right hand. Oh, shit. What did he have planned?

"Well, doll, we're going to do some experiments now. See if we can bring on the change. Shall we start with seeing if pain will do the trick?"

Swallowing, she looked him in the eye. "You already know pain won't do it. You hit me hard enough to knock me out. That hurt pretty fucking bad and would have accomplished whatever you think I can do."

Cringing, she leaned back, trying to get away from that blade. A gasp escaped her when the chair tilted, but before she went over, he slammed his free hand now clenched into a fist, down on her thigh, keeping her and the chair upright while deadening her leg. Her heart was beating out of control, and she opened her mouth to suck in more air. She couldn't seem to get enough into her lungs.

"Ahh, but we didn't draw blood now, did we? And quit cussing. It's unladylike."

She frowned at him as she shook her head in disbelief. He had an issue with her swearing, but was happy to carve her up? Light glinted off the blade, and she forgot all about his screwed-up morals.

Nathan! Help me! They've got a knife and they want to hurt me.

"I'll draw as much of the pain from your

mind as I can. I wish I could do more for you, Abigail, but this is all I can manage with the distance separating us."

She had no idea how Nathan would take the pain, or if he was even real, but she hoped it was true. Hoped that whether he was a real person who was telepathically in her mind or her imagination getting creative, her pain would be eased.

As the man roughly gripped her shoulder, her heart rate tripled until all she could hear was the pounding of her blood in her ears. When he pinned her against the back of the chair, she tried to lower her shoulder to get out of his grip, but it was no use. His hold held firm.

Her scream echoed around her as the sharp knife sliced deep into the flesh of her upper breast. Every muscle in her body went tight as she panted through the red-hot agony that burned her chest. She could feel Nathan's presence in her mind taking some of the pain and attempting to soothe her, but it still hurt like a bitch. How deep had he cut? The motion of the slice had been too smooth for it to have hit bone, but she wasn't sure. It wasn't like she was familiar with being hacked up by lunatics.

"Well, guess that doesn't do the trick, does

it? Patch her up enough to stop her from bleeding out, but make it quick."

Bleeding out? Oh, fuck. She was going to die in this room. This sadistic bastard was going to torture her until she ran out of blood and died. Sweat broke out over her flesh as heat flashed through her. She trembled as she continued to struggle to breathe. She watched the guy who'd brought her water approach her with a solemn expression and a packet of some kind. He bent to her and, without looking her in the eye, pressed several Steri-strips over the long cut. She winced and groaned with each one he laid against her. She doubted those little things would hold such a deep cut closed for long. Maybe they just wanted another excuse to hurt her.

"Hmmm, what to try next?"

Tears blurred her vision as he picked up and put down several items on the table. The sound of metal scraping made her teeth tingle, and she clenched her jaw against it.

"Electricity often does the trick in the movies. Let's give that a go, shall we?"

She whimpered when he turned to face her holding a Taser. Tears leaked down her face. There was no stopping them at this point. She hoped like hell this shit worked and she could turn into a bird and fly away because if it didn't, she really didn't want to think about what they might try next.

As soon as the other man moved away, the nasty one came back in close. She tested her bonds again, desperate to escape, but they still held strong. She clenched her jaw and tensed her muscles as he pressed the little black box against her bare thigh just below the edge of her shorts.

The electricity burned through her whole body, rattling her mind to the point she couldn't think, and every one of her joints felt loose from being shaken so badly. When her mind finally refocused, her ears were ringing, and pain thundered in her thigh. Her throat was parched from screaming, and her body hung loose in her bonds. She couldn't hold herself up—nothing worked. Couldn't the bastard just kill her already?

"What did they just do to you, Abigail?"

"Taser."

"Bloody monsters."

Yep, they certainly were. She had no energy and was struggling to get her body to perform even the simplest of functions, like breathing regularly. She didn't have the capacity to focus well enough to talk with

Nathan beyond the one word she'd managed to push at him.

With her head hanging forward and her hair covering her face, she didn't see him coming until she felt the heat. Then the intense agony as her skin melted.

"Fuck!"

Her head jerked back as her whole body tightened. This was more pain than she'd ever experienced, and she found herself wishing for death just so it would end.

She glanced to the side to see what they'd used on her and shuddered at the sight of flames licking up her arm. She flipped her head to get her hair away from the blow torch. Last thing she needed was her hair to catch and her head ending up engulfed in fire. For her to still be conscious, she knew Nathan must be taking a fair amount of the pain from her, but the agony was still incredibly debilitating. She panted as tears streamed down her face. Black spots began to crowd her vision, and she reached for the darkness, craving the peace unconsciousness would hopefully bring, whether it was for a few minutes or eternity. She didn't care, so long as the agony stopped.

Shivering, she woke gasping. Her body was submerged in water, the cool liquid such a stark contrast to the heat she'd endured before passing out. A firm hand on either shoulder pushed her down until her face was beneath the surface. Her mind whirled with panic, but she managed to still her lungs before she breathed in any water. The moment the pressure let up, she clenched her stomach muscles and forced herself into a sitting position, sputtering and gasping for air.

When would this hell end?

Agony burned from her thigh and arm along with a strong pounding in her head. She gulped a couple breaths before she found herself being pushed under water once more.

They were trying to drown her. Her mind split. Part of her wanted to fight. To thrash and do whatever it took to escape. The other part wanted to give up, just wanting the pain to end.

"Don't you dare give up, Abigail. Your males are coming. They'll be there any moment now. Just hang on, if not for yourself, for them."

"I'm drowning!"

"Focus and hold your breath. Release a little at a time to give yourself longer. You need to calm your heart rate and focus solely on your breathing. When they let you up, take deep

breaths with your nose, and fill your lungs right up."

When the pressure disappeared again, she repeated the process of sitting up as fast as she could. They'd bound her hands in front of her, so she was completely reliant on her stomach muscles to hold her up. She gulped more air before remembering Nathan's advice and focused on taking deep breaths. Her heart was pounding so hard, she was certain it had bruised the muscles surrounding it. When hands gripped her shoulders again, she screamed and thrashed all she could. Couldn't they see none of this crap was doing anything but hurting her?

A hard slap echoed around the room a moment before stinging pain ran up the side of her face.

"Shut up, bitch! You're stirring up the birds."

Shock stilled her movements. Birds? Silently, she raised her bound hands to grip the side of the old bathtub she was in to look around the new room. A shiver ran through her as the cool air touched her wet skin and clothes. It was too cold to be above ground. Looking up, the dirt ceiling confirmed that she was indeed underground.

Her heart lurched when she glanced to the left. The entire wall was lined with cages, huge metal things that contained beautiful, big eagles. Each of them was going nuts, head butting the rails and throwing their bodies around, trying to break free. For her? Were they upset for her? She wondered if they could hear her like Nathan could.

Squinting, she focused on them and pushed calming thoughts their way. No words, just wide-open skies and freedom with a gentle, soothing breeze. The birds began to calm and the noise in the room lowered instantly. She let her body go loose against the side of the tub as lethargy took over. She was so worn out and in so much pain she could barely hold onto a thought.

"How did you do that?"

Dammit. That had been a mistake. If she'd been able to think clearly, she wouldn't have risked trying to calm them. Maybe she could play it off that she hadn't helped them. "Do what?"

"Shut them up."

"I stopped screaming like you said. Guess they didn't like all the noise."

"Bullshit!"

She heard his footfalls get closer, but she

didn't even have the energy left to tense up for whatever he was going to do.

"You're pissing me off with your refusal to tell me what you know. I know you did something just now. And it looks like we have time for one last little test before we have to go. How about we see what a broken bone does for you?"

More? She was one hundred percent sure he knew it wouldn't work. No, he was simply pissed off with her for not giving him what he wanted and was lashing out. She whimpered and her body tensed as he dragged her roughly from the tub onto the dirt. She landed hard, jarring her body and setting off a new round of pain. Would this torture never end?

three

If eagles could speak, Kane would be cursing. Frustration hardened his stomach. He'd never had worse luck when out flying. Not only had he not managed to catch a damn thermal, but he was also heading into a strong crosswind, and it was taking forever to get to the location Jeremy had shown him. At least it would be a tailwind for his twin, so he'd make good time to their destination.

He prayed this place was where Abigail was being held. His every muscle was tired and ready to collapse from exhaustion.

"How close are you?"

He wasn't surprised to hear his twin's voice, or the fact that he sounded panicked. Kane wasn't certain exactly how much time had passed since Abigail had been taken, but it had to be hours.

"Not sure. Ten minutes, maybe? This wind is killing me."

"Has Nathan spoken to you?"

"Not since I left. Why?"

"Nathan managed to connect with her, Kane. They're torturing her, bro."

Pain ripped through his heart, making it hard to keep flapping his wings. He dipped lower for a moment before he forced his body to function.

"What the fuck? So it is the crazies?"

Adrenaline flowed through his veins, giving him a second wind. He made the most of it and powered forward as fast as he could.

"Yes, it's the crazies, and they're stepping things up. Nathan is sending an ambulance to the location I found. Now that he's connected with her, he's certain we have the right place."

"I can see eagles circling up ahead. Know anything about that?"

"Nathan didn't mention them, he just told me to hurry the hell up."

"They're circling a building. The car's been uncovered. Oh, hell, no. These bastards are not getting away."

Stretching his lean body out to make himself more aerodynamic, he dove as fast as he could toward the building. His Abigail had to still be alive. Anything else they could deal with, he just needed her to still be with them in the land of the living. As he got closer, he saw a body lying next to the car.

"Jer, I've got one dead outside. Looks like the eagles took him down while he was trying to escape."

"I can see the circling birds too. I'll be there soon."

With his wings spread wide to slow his descent, Kane landed near the rear of the house. He quickly shifted, thankful that left him wearing what he'd had on before he'd taken on his eagle form, then slipped inside the door. The smell within was horrendous. Burnt flesh and fresh blood filled his senses and had him barely resisting the urge to vomit.

He silently moved through the old, ruined house, finding no one. When he slipped into the kitchen, his pulse quickened and he clenched his fists, wishing he could pound into whoever was responsible for what was in front of him. A wooden chair sat in the center of the room and there was blood splattered around it. Taking a deep breath, he shut down his rage. It wouldn't help him get Abigail free. Looking around, he finally spotted the small entry to a basement. Most of these old houses had at least one small underground room. It had been the only way in the old days that they could find some level of coolness in the summer months.

Another man lay dead to the side of the entrance. It looked like he'd tried to run away, but the eagles had attacked him. Kane swiftly climbed down the stairs and found himself in his worst nightmare. His precious Abigail lay out cold on the floor. Her arms were stretched out, and her bound hands rested on a lever that had opened a wall of cages. His heart ached and he swallowed past a lump in his throat. She looked so broken. He rushed to her side, breathing her name, praying she was still alive.

He gently rolled her onto her back and moved the wet tangle of hair away from her face and neck. His breath caught at the damage done to her as he pressed two fingers to her pulse point under her jaw. Her skin was warm, and a sluggish beat pumped against his digits. His body slumped a moment in relief that she was alive.

"Where are you?"

"Head to the old kitchen and down the stairs. Bring a first aid kit if you can find one anywhere, and a knife."

He ran his gaze down her body. A deep slash marred the top curve of her right breast and blood had soaked most of her tank top. Her left arm was charred from the elbow to the shoulder. Fury and agony mixed within him, and heated his blood as he imagined what she'd suffered. Her thigh had a nasty burn on it just above her knee and her lower right leg had been broken. It lay at an unnatural angle, and her skin was marred with bruises. All her clothing was saturated, and beads of water covered her skin. He'd seen the old bathtub when he'd first scanned the room. He could only imagine what they'd tried to do to her.

"Oh, fuck. Nathan warned me, but still..."

Struggling to breathe, Kane looked up as Jeremy dropped to his knees on Abigail's other side.

"She's so broken, Jer. They fucked her up bad. How will she ever recover from it all?" He carefully cradled her hands in his own as Jeremy cut the rope off her, revealing more bruises.

"With our help. We'll make sure she makes a full recovery. No way will the elders make us wait for her to be of age after this. We'll bond with her and make sure she's protected twenty-four-seven. Nothing like this will ever happen to her again."

Kane opened a telepathic connection to

Nathan and Jeremy so his twin could hear what they said.

"Nathan, how far away is that ambulance? Abigail is really messed up."

"It's coming from Marree, so it should be there any moment. Abigail is still alive? I was worried when my connection to her dropped."

"She's out cold. Her arm's burned badly, as is her thigh. Her lower right leg is broken, and she's been sliced on her chest."

"I know, Kane. I was in her mind when they injured her. I took as much of the pain as I could. Then helped her free the captured eagles when they finally left her unattended."

"Do we have clan permission to bond with her? Once she's healed enough, can we forego the need for her to be twenty-one?"

"I've told her what she is and who you both are to her. There's no reason for you to hold off now. But she must consent, you can't just take her. I suspect after this ordeal, you'll have your work cut out to convince her."

A siren blared through the silence, and Kane was grateful when Jeremy rose to jog up the stairs. His shoulders slumped forward in weariness. Now that the adrenaline had left Kane's system, his muscles didn't want to do much of anything. Except for his heart. That ached as he stared at his sweet, broken Abigail.

Several sets of boots stomped overhead before coming down the stairs. It didn't take long for the small basement to become crowded. Two paramedics and two cops had rushed down following Jeremy. His twin grabbed him by the shoulders and when Kane's legs refused to cooperate, Jeremy had to basically lift him to his feet so he could stumble away from Abigail to let the medics work on her.

"Can either of you tell me what happened here?"

Taking a deep breath, Kane forced his gaze away from his mate and faced the middle-aged cop. Grateful it was one who knew of their kind, he kept the story short.

"After Abigail was snatched this afternoon, we went looking for her. We were only fifteen minutes behind them, but it still took us until a little while ago to find her here. We turned up to find two dead men and Abigail down here, out cold."

"Okay, we'll wait for Abigail to regain consciousness for her statement to get a full picture of what happened, but it looks like it'll be an open and shut case. She was taken by two men, both of which are now dead from animal attacks. I doubt we'll have too much more to do with the case and be able to leave you all in peace fairly quickly."

"Not so simple, I'm afraid. There were at least three people in that car that took her. But we saw no sign of the third person when we arrived and searched."

"We'll look into that side of things. If they've taken off through the outback, they'll fall victim to the elements."

"I don't suppose you could give us a lift to the hospital?"

"Sorry, boys. Normally we could, but we need to go looking for that other kidnapper. I'll chat with the medics and see if they can't fit you in."

Kane rubbed his palm over the back of his neck. He knew the ambulance wasn't big enough for them both to travel in the back alongside Abigail, and he really didn't have the energy to fly again today, so he hoped the medics would let them sit in the front or something.

The cop cupped his shoulder and gave him a tight squeeze. "Don't look so worried, we'll get you both there somehow."

With Jeremy all but carrying him, they

trudged up the stairs behind the medics as they carried Abigail on a stretcher to the waiting ambulance.

He hoped she didn't push them away like Nathan had hinted she would.

Abigail clenched her fingers into fists before stretching them out straight. Taking a deep breath, she opened her eyes and focused on her reflection. It had been nearly two months since her abduction, and earlier today she'd finally had the cast taken off her broken leg. As soon as she'd gotten home, she hurried to her room to be alone so she could strip down to her underwear and take in the horror that was her new body. A lump formed in her throat. Her scars were hideous. Tears pricked her eyes when she traced the smooth pink line that curved over the top of her right breast. That scar had forever ended her ability to wear the low-cut tops and dresses she'd always loved. Maybe once it faded to silver-white, she could cover it with makeup and occasionally wear one of her favourite dresses. She took a deep, shaky breath. It would be a long time before that would happen.

The skin grafts to her arm had helped, but the skin was still gruesome. That bastard had seared from her elbow up to her shoulder with his bloody blow torch. She was certain she would never be able to look at one again without shuddering. Her gaze dropped to her legs, taking the right one in for the first time since she'd been injured.

The electrical burn on her left thigh she'd already seen. Not as severe as her arm, it was still repulsive to look at. Her right calf had surgical scars from where they'd opened her up to fix her leg. Apparently, her being a shifter meant they couldn't do what they normally did with screws and plates. Thankfully, they had several shifter-friendly staff at the local hospital that knew what to do. They'd explained to her how that would have ended badly when she would eventually shift forms. So, they had gone in, cleaned up the bone fragments and realigned it all, then set it in plaster and put her on bed rest until it healed. At least with her shifter genetics, the bone regenerated relatively quickly. Pity the scars didn't heal over. Every book she'd ever read said shifters were perfection. Never scarring, their wounds always healed seamlessly. She let out a huff and wiped at her tears. Trust that bit to be the false part.

"Sweetheart?"

"Yeah, Mum? I'm in here."

Her mother had been there holding her hand when they'd cut off the plaster. She'd seen all her daughter's new horrors, so Abigail didn't bother trying to cover up.

"Oh, my baby girl. Don't cry."

She hadn't meant to, but her tear ducts weren't listening.

"How can I not? Look at me. No one will ever want me now."

Her mother wrapped her arms around her and pulled her in for a hug.

"Oh, don't be silly. Any boy that can only see the wrapping isn't worth your time. A true man will see your heart and soul and love every piece of you."

Jeremy and Kane hadn't strayed far from her since she'd woken in hospital. But, so far, she hadn't built up the courage to talk to them. Nathan had called them her "destined mates," but did that mean they didn't have a choice? Did they have to put up with her now that she was ugly, even though they'd no doubt prefer to go find some other perfect shifter who was still whole? A shudder ran through her. She didn't feel whole anymore.

Her adoptive parents weren't shifters. They didn't appear to know anything about her true world. Since her attack, Nathan had visited several times and attempted to explain things, but she was struggling to wrap her mind around any of it. What she did understand was that Kane and Jeremy wouldn't touch or speak to her until she said she was ready for them to.

Whenever they were close, her skin prickled with awareness, so she knew how often they'd been nearby, but they'd stayed out of sight mostly and seemed content to keep her protected from a distance. *Probably because they can't stand the sight of me up close anymore.*

"Those Gibson twins still seem pretty keen."

With a gasp, she pulled back from her mother's embrace. She knew?

"Oh, don't look so shocked, sweetheart. Nathan sat us down when we first adopted you and explained who you were and what could happen when you were older in regard to who you'd end up marrying."

"And you and Dad are fine with that?"

One of the reasons she hadn't spoken with

the twins was that she was still grappling with the concept of having two men.

"Well, of course, we would have preferred a normal one-on-one coupling for you, but it was Kane and Jeremy who brought you back to us. They searched non-stop from the moment they found out you'd been taken. It was Jeremy who spotted the old house on satellite feed. How can we not approve of two men who are so clearly devoted to you?"

Frustration built within her. "But I'm not the same girl I was before! I don't want a man, or two, who are only with me because fate or destiny or some higher power is forcing them. I can just imagine how they'll cringe when they see me naked. What kind of intimacy will I have with men who cringe, Mum?"

Her mother cupped her face in her warm palms, and she leaned into the contact.

"You're making an awful lot of assumptions, sweetheart. You won't know for sure until it happens, but from what the police told me, those men have seen your scars at their worst, just after they happened, while you were unconscious. And you know what they did?"

The tension seeped out of her shoulders. "They demanded they go with me to the hospital."

"That's right. They convinced the medics to break protocol and allow them both to travel with you, and at least one of them has been near you since. Think about that for a moment, Abigail. They run that garage by themselves. They are pulling some seriously long hours between keeping you protected and all their work over there."

Heat burned her cheeks, and she squeezed her eyes closed. How could she be so inconsiderate to them?

"I hadn't thought of that. I didn't mean to be so selfish."

"Oh, you're not being selfish, sweetheart. You've been through one hell of an ordeal and survived it. They understand you need time. Just promise me you'll give them a chance before you write them off."

"I promise. I'll talk with them."

"Don't leave them waiting too long, sweetheart."

Her mother pressed a kiss to her forehead before she headed out the door, leaving her alone. She stumbled over to sit on her bed. What was she going to do? She didn't know how to handle the twins, let alone be brave enough to go to them, to find a way so they didn't have to work so hard.

four

His spanner slipped and fire raced up his arm when his knuckles slammed against the hard metal of the truck.

"Fuck!"

Jeremy continued to curse as he moved to stand and inspect his injured hand.

"You okay?"

He forgot all about his stupid injury the second he heard her voice. Abigail had sought him out? Was she finally ready to give them a chance?

"Abigail? That you, baby?"

He winced. Of course, it was her. No one else's voice sounded as sweet as his Abigail's. He snatched up a rag to wrap around his bleeding knuckles as he walked around the side of the truck toward the open front roller door. He grinned when he spotted her slowly coming toward him. She looked adorable in her ankle-length flowing skirt and long-sleeved top. He already knew she'd had her cast taken off earlier today. It was Kane's shift on guard duty, so his twin had followed her in and back from the hospital. Now she was walking with a cane and a slight limp. But she was up and around. He'd been so worried her leg wouldn't heal correctly. especially since he knew the doctor wouldn't have been able to use the normal screws and plates on her. He wondered if it would affect her eagle. The burst of magic required to shift forms was supposed to help heal any injuries, but he'd never tested the theory.

"It's great to see you up and around. How's your leg feeling?"

She was frowning at his hand as she hobbled over to him. Mesmerized, he stood still and admired her form as she approached him.

"Feels weird to have it out in the air, but to be up walking around without everybody panicking about me re-injuring myself feels great. How's your hand?"

"It's fine. Just scraped my knuckles. It's nothing."

His breathing picked up speed along with his heart rate when she came right up to him.

She picked his injured hand up, carefully unwrapping the rag before hissing in a breath.

"You've taken a fair bit of skin off. Probably should put some ice on them or something."

He grinned at her concern. She was so cute, playing nurse when she clearly had no idea what she was doing.

"Nah, they'll stop bleeding in a bit. Just need to keep a little pressure on it. Ice is for bruising, and since my hands are used to being scratched up like this, they don't need much attention."

Her soft skin felt so good against his, but he knew how dirty he was. Since he really wanted to be able to touch her, he needed to clean up fast.

"How about you head into the office, baby? I'll just go wash up and be there in a minute. I don't want to get grease all over you."

"Um, yeah okay. Well, I actually came over to ask if I could join you for lunch." She released his hand and re-gripped her stick before she turned and looked toward the roller door. "I know Kane was following me, and I thought he might like to join us too."

A weight lifted from his chest, and he grinned broadly as his brother slipped around the edge of the doorway and into her line of sight. She wanted to spend a whole meal with them? Today was definitely looking up.

"And here I thought I was being careful to not let you see me."

"Technically, I didn't see you, Kane. Mum told me how you're both taking turns keeping a constant guard on me. Although, I did often catch glimpses of one of you, I'd just put it down to my imagination."

Jeremy cocked a brow in curiosity. "Imagination?"

Her cheeks darkened with a blush, and she fumbled with her stick. "So, did you want lunch or not?"

Jeremy didn't fight the urge to grin like an idiot. Their little mate had been thinking about them enough to think she'd imagined seeing them.

"Have you been dreaming of us, honey?" Kane's query proved they were on the same page.

"Ahh, your place is adjoins this building, doesn't it? Is there an internal door?"

Oh, she was doing her best to avoid admitting anything, but Jeremy was determined to at least getting her to confess she'd been thinking about them. He strolled up to her and with a single finger, tilted her face up to his.

"I can tell you right now that we both sure as hell dream of you every damn night." He brushed his other thumb over her cheek, leaving a gray smudge over the red. "Is this blush because you've been doing the same with us, baby?"

She stared blankly at him for a few moments before she blinked and pulled her face free.

"I came over here to see you both, didn't I? Surely, that tells you everything you need to know."

Happy to have his answer, he turned his attention to Kane. "You right to go on ahead with Abigail?"

"Why can't we wait for you and go together?"

He liked that she wanted them both close to her, because that was where they both wanted to be. "Baby, along with scrubbing this grease off my hands, I need to close up the shop and hang up the out for lunch sign. I won't be long. No point in you standing out here risking getting that pretty skirt dirty if you don't have to."

"Oh. All right."

Another blush crept up her neck and Jeremy couldn't resist leaning in and kissing her cheek. "You are too sweet. Go on with Kane now, and we'll have us some lunch."

As Kane lead her toward the office where the adjourning door to their house was, Jeremy sprinted to the wash station to scrub his hands and forearms, trying to clean off as much grease as possible as quickly as he could. Their Abigail had finally come to them, and he didn't want to wait another moment to be near her.

By the time he got the roller door shut and the sign out, his hands were trembling with excitement. Not wanting to waste a second, he pulled his shirt over his head as he entered their house. A glance down confirmed he really should change his pants too. If he got the opportunity to get that close to her, he'd take it, and he didn't want to cover her in grease and oil. Their place had been designed with the laundry room between the house and garage so they could strip out of their dirty work gear before entering their home. He laid his shirt and pants on the washing machine so he could change back into them afterwards. On silent feet, he slipped into the hallway and on to his bedroom where he snatched up a pair of cargo shorts. He pulled them on then walked down toward the kitchen where he could hear Kane and Abigail chatting about her rehab.

As he sat on the barstool beside Abigail, Kane slid a plate in front of him and another in front of their girl before he served himself and sat on her other side. They ate in comfortable silence for a few minutes before Jeremy's curiosity got the better of him.

"So, aside from some food, was there something you wanted us for, Abigail?"

The garage was backed up with work due to all the time he and Kane were taking off to protect her, so unfortunately, he couldn't afford to spend the entire afternoon encouraging her to reveal what she'd come to them for. He needed to work out what she was ready for and fast. But he winced in regret when she looked up at him like a kangaroo caught in headlights. She flicked her gaze between him and Kane as she gripped the bench with a white-knuckled grip. His heart took a dive. He'd never forgive himself if he'd just pushed her too hard and she ran from them.

"I have no idea how or where to start this conversation. Um, I guess I should begin by saying thank you. I'm sure I haven't heard all you did for me that day, but I know it was the two of you who found and saved me, so thank you for that."

Still feeling a little guilty for making our poor girl so nervous, Jeremy tried to ease the mood with some humour.

"What? Not even a thank you kiss? We just get the words? I don't know if that's fair, baby. What do you think, Kane? Think we deserve a little kiss in gratitude?"

"Hell, yeah. Any excuse will suit me fine."

A blush crept over her cheeks once more, but she smiled and chuckled a little. "Guess that's a fair request, considering all you did."

She turned in her seat to face Jeremy, and he followed her lead. Her eyes widened as she took in his bared chest. Automatically, his shoulders went straight, and he puffed up a little under her scrutiny. She tentatively put her hand on his shoulder, and he did his best to contain the shudder that ran through his body. The feel of her skin against his made a flash of arousal roll through him. He stilled when she leaned in and pressed her lips softly against his cheek. This time, he didn't bother holding back his reaction. He let her feel the shiver that passed through him at her gentle touch. When she went to pull back, he slid his hand up to the nape of her neck to hold her close.

"I want a real kiss, baby."

His heart pounded as he leaned in to rub his lips over her soft ones twice before he covered her mouth with his and kissed her like he'd always dreamed of doing. She moved closer to him, sliding from her seat and making a place for herself between his thighs. He groaned when her softness came into contact with his rock-hard erection. If it felt this good through layers of clothing, he could only imagine how mindless it would send him to have her naked against him.

She opened her lips with a gasp, and he made the most of the opportunity, swiping his tongue into her mouth. She tasted divine. He rested his other hand over her hip as he continued his exploration of her sexy little mouth. When her body trembled and she moaned, he pulled back to see Kane had shifted his stool and moved in behind her. He was pressing his lips where her neck and shoulder joined.

Jeremy slid his hand from her nape, stroking gently down the side of her body until he had both palms on her hips. He grinned when Kane kissed his way up to her jaw before he tilted her face his way and captured her mouth. They both moaned, and Jeremy felt the shiver that passed through her body.

He hesitated as a wave of trepidation crashed over him. Could he believe this? That she'd simply walked over here and fell in their laps? Jeremy didn't want to be the devil's advocate, but he wanted forever with Abigail, not just a short fling. He had to make sure she knew what she was starting with them.

"Kane, back off. We need to sort out some things before we get any more heated up."

Jeremy was careful to keep his voice projected to his twin alone. He didn't want stray words filtering through to Abigail and giving her the wrong idea. Kane slowed his kiss before he finally released her.

"Hmm, you can thank me any time you like, honey, if that's how you say it."

Jeremy's hands dropped from her as she turned her body into Kane's and leaned up to nibble on his jaw. She was clearly looking for more of his kisses. Kane flashed Jeremy a desperate look with a raised eyebrow.

"Can't we just take her to bed?"

"Not yet. We do that, we'll end up bonding with her. What if she has second thoughts and tries to leave us? And what about our plans? No.

We need to take a little time and make sure we do this right."

Jeremy ran a hand over the soft skin of her waist, slipping under her loose-fitting shirt so he could feel the smoothness of her lower back. He encouraged her to turn so she could see them both.

"Abigail, talk to us, baby. What brought you over here today?"

She chewed on her lower lip and frowned deeply. "Nathan told me what you both are to me."

Relaxing, he smiled gently to encourage her. He had a good idea where she was going with this conversation now. "What'd he say?"

"That you're both my destined mates."

Jeremy wondered if he should thank his elder or curse him for that little favour. "And did he explain that in more detail for you?"

"Just that once we *bond*, I'll be able to shift form."

Kane caressed her cheek and she leaned into him. "Why'd it take you two months to stop pushing us away?"

"I'm not who I was. I'm a mess. My body is scarred so badly, and I don't sleep much..." Her voice trailed off.

Jeremy frowned. He hadn't known about

her having trouble sleeping. How he wished they were already bonded. If she were sleeping between him and Kane, she wouldn't have nightmares. They'd both be there to make sure of it.

"You having nightmares, baby? Have you told your doctor?"

"Of course, I'm having nightmares, Jeremy! I was tortured, dammit. I'm broken now!"

She pulled from their touch, taking a step away. His heart ached as she wrapped her arms around her middle. His fingers itched with the need to snatch her back so she was between them where they could comfort her. But he couldn't. At least not yet. She needed to say what she'd come here to say, then they would soothe her and show her it was all going to be okay.

"Neither of you can possibly still want me. You're just doing what you have to because fate or some higher power is forcing you to."

Tears streamed down her cheeks, and Jeremy's heart shattered for her. Unable to resist a moment longer, he stood, scooped her up in his arms, and headed to the couch in the lounge room. He sat with her on his lap and a lump formed in his throat when she curled into him. Kane sat beside him, placing her legs over his lap while she pressed her ear over Jeremy's heart and sniffled. Needing to touch her, he ran his hand through her thick hair, stroking her while he spoke.

"Let's get some things straight, baby. No one, human or otherwise, made us fall for you. We've been drawn to you for years and our affection for you grew over time. We may not have spoken to you beyond small talk at the roadhouse, or taken you out on dates, but we were always there. Watching, waiting. Did Nathan explain what we are? That we have extra rules to follow?"

She nodded against him, her hair tickling as she moved. "He said you're Wedge-tailed eagle shifters, and that you weren't allowed to bond with me until after I turned twenty-one."

"That's right and trust me, we had all sorts of plans for you after you turned twenty-one. After you were taken, we asked, and the elders gave us permission to bypass the age restriction. We don't have to wait anymore to tell you how we feel. Destiny may have brought you to be adopted by Paul and Carol out here where you met us, and it might offer its approval of our union. But even if we were solely human with no supernatural elements to contend with, we'd want you. You're beautiful inside and out, Abigail. You always will be."

He winced when she shuddered and a sob escaped. He hadn't meant to upset her.

"Not anymore. Others are prettier. Those bastards said all shifters were beautiful. You both could leave me and go find someone perfect. Someone you'd be proud of."

She was breaking his heart. Did she really see herself that way? Jeremy couldn't speak and was grateful when Kane leaned in and cupped her cheek in his palm before he spoke.

"Abigail, we don't need to go looking elsewhere when we have perfection right here. I know you have scars, honey. We all do. Some people have them only on the inside, some on the outside, and some have both. But that doesn't make you any less than exactly who we want and need."

Jeremy pressed a kiss to the top of her head. "Yep, you're scarred perfection, baby, and we'd both be proud to call you ours and show you off."

She pressed against Kane's palm, seeking their touch even as she continued to argue, "You don't even know what you're calling beautiful. Neither of you have seen how badly I'm scarred from the injuries. They're really bad. I'm not sure I'll be able to handle you cringing when you see them."

Didn't she realize they'd seen her injuries when they found her? That they'd seen them before her wounds had been cleaned and tended to, before the skin grafts?

"We would never do that to you. Let us prove it. Choose a scar to show us right now."

Abigail looked from Jeremy's serious eyes to Kane's. They both seemed so solemn as they waited for her. Swallowing down her nerves, she leaned away from Jeremy's muscular chest. Lying against him with her ear pressed over his heart had helped calm her more than she'd thought it would. There was something soothing about the strong, regular beat of his heart. Biting her lower lip, she started to pull her shirt up. Her bra covered everything important, and she knew her arm and breast would test their resolve. She slammed her eyes shut before the material passed over her head. No matter how much she wanted to see their reaction, she couldn't bring herself to open her eyes. She was petrified of what she'd see in their gazes.

"Look at us, baby. Don't ever be afraid with us."

When Kane lifted her legs from his lap and got up, her eyes popped open as her heart shattered. He was leaving. She'd wanted them to prove her wrong, not confirm her very worst fears. Maybe she shouldn't have come over here today...it was too soon. Emotion clogged her throat as Kane lowered himself to kneel by her side. He trailed a single fingertip down the inside of her arm, next to the fresh, ugly red scarring.

"Oh, honey. I'm so sorry this happened to you. It must have hurt like a mother."

"Nathan took some of the pain from me."

"Would you tell us what happened? But only if you want to. It might help you move past it."

She sighed and curled up against Jeremy's muscular chest again, and he lifted a hand to tenderly trace the scar on her breast with a callused fingertip. A wave of relief flowed through her. Neither had turned her away or rejected her. Somehow, that acceptance loosened her tongue, allowing words to tumble out before she thought better of it.

"They wanted me to shift to an eagle. When I said I didn't know what they were on about, they tried to force me to change. Until Nathan started speaking to me, I thought they were complete nutjobs."

"They are, baby. We call them the crazies for a reason."

She smiled a little. The title fit them, that was for sure. With a deep breath, she wet her lips before confessing the first injury. "First they tried by making me bleed." She covered Jeremy's hand with her own. "Here."

"Someone had tried to patch it up before we found you."

"Yeah, one of the men did that. He gave me water to drink in the beginning. He was the one that got away. The police haven't been able to find him, but I doubt he'll cause any trouble, assuming he survived the outback. He was the one who convinced the others to leave me with just my hands tied, which enabled me to free the birds."

Figuring she may as well get this whole reveal-the-horror-show done and dusted here and now, she reached down and pulled her skirt up above her knees.

"Electricity was next on their torture-the-innocent list. I had shorts on, so he pressed the Taser here, just above my knee."

"Fuck."

Jeremy's voice was raw, and she could feel the fury radiating from him. Kane lowered his face and pressed a kiss to the puckered flesh and her heart lurched. Her scars truly didn't repulse them? Dare she believe it?"

"Heat was next. They used a blow torch on my arm. You know the small battery ones people use to cook with? I passed out during that one. I woke up with them attempting to drown me. The last thing they did was take a hammer to my leg. I don't think that was really a test. Pretty sure they were just pissed off with me for not doing what they wanted.

"After they broke my leg, they left me on the dirt floor with my hands tied. Nathan was still in my mind, and it was he that took my pain long enough for me to drag myself over to release the latch on the cages. After that, I passed out. I have no idea what happened from then until I woke up in the hospital."

"But someone has told you what happened, right?"

"Yes, the police told me. So, now you've both seen my little freak show. You sure you don't want to run the other way while you still can? I won't hold it against you if you do."

She rubbed her cheek against Jeremy's chest, loving how his hot flesh felt against her own. She hoped they wouldn't take her up on her offer and walk away from her. What she knew of them, she liked, and she loved how it felt to be held by Jeremy in his lap.

"I think we should get her hearing checked, Kane."

"Definitely. She sure does seem to be having trouble listening to us."

Jeremy's arms tightened around her.

"I heard you both just fine. I can't help that I'm having trouble believing it."

"Maybe a physical demonstration would help."

Butterflies fluttered in her belly when Kane followed his words with kisses over her shoulder. He trailed his fingers up over her bra strap and gently pulled it down, holding it up over her skin so it wouldn't scrape her scarred flesh, until it hung loosely around her elbow. Jeremy moved her off his chest and cupped her face. His kiss scorched her all the way to her soul. When Kane peeled her bra cup down away from her breast, cool air brushed over her nipple a moment before wet heat enveloped it.

She arched into him as he suckled her. Her body hummed, wanting more. Jeremy left her mouth and pulled the other strap down. He peeled away her bra to reveal her other breast, and a moan escaped her when he rubbed his thumb over her peak, his eyes heating as it hardened for him. She whimpered and rubbed her legs together in an attempt to relieve the arousal that was tightening her lower belly and demanding attention.

She was suddenly chilled when they both moved away, but before she could protest, Jeremy lifted her to stand with her back to his front. Kane stood before her, breathing hard and nearly setting her on fire with the heat in his gaze. Jeremy moved her hair over her shoulder, and her skin tingled as his callused fingers moved over her back, freeing the clasp on her bra. With her arms down at her sides, it instantly fell to the floor and Kane groaned. Instinctively, she raised her palms to cover herself, conscious that they were small and not full or round like men wanted.

"Don't you dare. These are ours, and you don't hide them from us."

He cupped one in each hand, gently kneading her, and she leaned back against Jeremy as her body turned boneless.

"Fuck. Look at that, Jeremy. She's a sweet handful. Just perfect."

"That she is."

She opened her mouth to call them liars,

but Kane took her lips in a kiss powerful enough it blurred her thoughts until all that remained was her desire for these two men. The slide of material over her hips had her trembling against Kane. Aside from her sandals, she was completely naked between them now.

Heat flashed over her cheeks when Jeremy stepped back a moment before lips pressed against her right ass cheek. A masculine chuckle filled the air as she was lowered onto Jeremy's lap. Her spine pressed against his chest, and she hummed at the tingles that passed through her. His large hands came around to cup her breasts as Kane had done earlier. He kneaded then tugged gently on her nipples until she was squirming against him.

When Kane dropped to his knees and gripped each of hers, she gasped and looked down at him. With a smile filled with male satisfaction, he hooked her calves over Jeremy's legs before Jeremy widened them, spreading her thighs and revealing every inch of her to Kane's view. Heat raced over her body, and she knew she was blushing all over. But before she could move to cover herself, Kane ran his palms up the insides of her thighs, sending spikes of arousal straight to her core.

"You're gorgeous, honey. Will you let me have a taste? I'll stop the moment you tell me to, but I'm dying to know what it's like to have your taste on my tongue."

He rubbed small circles over her inner thighs as he waited for her answer. Jeremy sucked gently at a tender spot on her throat, and she gave in to the arousal and desire coursing through her.

"Please, Kane. I ache."

five

Kane couldn't quite believe he had Abigail naked and willing before him. He briefly glanced up to his twin, who gave him a little smirk and a nod before he returned to nibbling on their mate's neck as he continued to play with her spectacular breasts. They sat perky and high on her chest and really were the sweetest handfuls. His fingers itched to touch them again. He was certain he'd never tire of playing with them. But right now, he had other places to explore.

With a growl, he lowered to nuzzle his nose in the crease between her torso and thigh. A shudder ran through him when he inhaled her scent deep within him. After he licked straight up her centre and her flavour exploded over his senses, he rested his forehead against her thigh for a moment to savour his first taste and enjoy the high it brought him.

"Delicious."

She trembled beneath him, and his mind spun as he moved back to take more of her within him. He wanted to watch her come for him. After another couple of long licks, he suckled her clit and worried it between his teeth. Her fingers slid into his hair, and she took a fistful as he moved down and thrust his tongue deep in her channel. Her walls clamped down on him, and he groaned. Heaven. She felt like heaven.

He couldn't wait to make love to her, to bond with her. She was tight and slick around him as he continued to mimic what he wanted to do with his dick. When he teased her clit with his thumb, she tightened around him with a whimper.

Slipping his other hand under her, he was grateful she'd wriggled forward, away from his brother's crotch. He pressed a finger over her back hole at the same time as he flicked her clit and preened with pride as she flew apart with a scream. He lapped at her gently as she gave up her cream to him until her body relaxed beneath him. Warmth radiated throughout his entire being. Sitting back on his heels, he wiped his face with his palm before licking it clean. He didn't want to waste a drop of her sweetness.

Jeremy whispered against her ear and lowered his hand down her torso. She groaned and arched against his fingers when he slipped them between her wet folds. Mesmerized, Kane watched as his twin stroked their mate. Her folds were flushed a dark pink and so wet he could hear the suction against his twin's digits. His erection throbbed against the zipper of his pants, and he rubbed the heel of his hand up and down his length a couple of times. They'd agreed they wouldn't take her until the bonding ceremony, but his dick wasn't liking that plan one bit, especially when she was spread before him all wet and willing. It would be so easy to unzip and slide within her tight channel.

Jeremy slid his glistening fingers free and brought them up to trace her lips with her cream. The sight was so erotic, Kane struggled to not come in his pants. Her gaze was locked onto Jeremy's, and she was panting. Damn, but Abigail was sexy as hell. Jeremy wasted no time in licking it off and kissing her deeply. Unable to simply keep watching, Kane leaned in and suckled a nipple into his mouth as he pressed his covered erection against her wetness, rubbing slowly against her.

She arched her hips up, and he wrapped his hand around her thigh when she lifted her uninjured leg around his waist. He caught a glimpse of Jeremy's arm shifting to slide between her ass cheeks, and she tensed when his twin began playing with her back entrance.

"What are you two doing to me?"

Her words were breathless and fed Kane's ego. He loved they could get her so hot so fast.

"We're giving you a little taste of what's to come, baby."

"And we're proving beyond a shadow of a doubt that we want you, honey. All of you."

He sped up his movements, moaning as his covered erection slid back and forth over her hard clit. With a scream, she threw her head back against Jeremy and came for them. The material of his shorts was instantly drenched with her cream and stuck to his aching length. With a few more strokes, he could do nothing but join her. With a yell, he shot off in his pants like a teen.

"Fuck!"

His shame lessened when his twin groaned, and by the scent in the air, had joined him in climaxing in his pants. He was glad he wasn't the only one who'd been unable to hold himself back. Kane slid his arm between her and Jeremy and pulled her tightly against him. With a hand cupped under her ass, he began to walk toward the bathroom. She slumped against him, apparently too worn out to care what he had planned for her. With her arms loosely wrapped around his shoulders, she licked the skin on his neck, causing goosebumps to rise on his flesh. She hummed when he gently set her on the bench in the bathroom. He stepped away to flick the shower on, and she gasped.

"Did I do that?"

He followed her gaze to look down at the mess on the front of his shorts.

"That was a joint effort, honey."

She looked mortified, and he couldn't help but laugh. He'd never been so happy, and she looked completely adorable, all rumpled and embarrassed.

"Don't look so horrified, baby. It'll wash off just fine."

She buried her face in her hands and her shoulders shook. All humour fled and concern took hold. He hadn't meant to upset her. He moved to stand between her thighs while he pulled her hands away. A lump formed in his throat when he saw that she was laughing *and* crying. How was he supposed to deal with that? Damn, women were weird.

"Come on, Abigail. Let's get you cleaned up and back home, so Jeremy can get back to work."

Slipping his hands beneath her ass, he boosted her up against him. With a small squeak, she clung to him as he moved her toward the shower.

"You carry me around so easily!"

"Compared to a car engine, you're as light as a feather, baby. And I love how you feel in my arms, so I'd suggest you get used to it."

He didn't mention the fact that eagle shifters liked to make love standing up, fully supporting their female's weight. He'd keep that surprise for their bonding.

Jeremy's voice boomed in the small space. "Wait!"

He stopped and turned to look at his twin. "What?"

"She still has her shoes on." As Jeremy slid her sandals free, he started chuckling, and soon the bathroom echoed with the sounds of all three of them laughing.

Moving the mouse, Abigail huffed while she watched the little arrow shift around the screen of her laptop. She should just let the thing go to sleep. It wasn't like she was getting any work done. After her attack, she'd opted to complete her classes online, but she'd struggled to focus on much while she was healing and was now so behind in basically every subject. She really needed to be studying today.

With another huff, she gave in to what she'd wanted to do all morning. Sitting forward, she glanced out the door of the office to the sight of the twins working. Kane was bent over, leaning into the engine bay of a car, his sexy butt in the air. Hmmm, that man filled out a pair of jeans perfectly. Jeremy's feet poked out from beneath the front of the vehicle. She could hear the low murmur of their deep, masculine voices, but couldn't pick up what they were saying.

She chewed on her lower lip. It'd been ten days since she'd marched over there and demanded lunch with them. After they'd cleaned up and headed back to the garage, she'd taken in all the vehicles waiting to be repaired. Guilt had swamped her. Even more so when she focused on the twins' faces and saw the lines of tiredness and stress that hadn't been there before her abduction. How had she not noticed that because they were spending so much time guarding her, they had been forced to neglect their business?

She'd stormed off across the road, gathered up her laptop, and told her parents she'd be studying in the twins' office from now on. It was all worth it the moment she'd turned and seen Jeremy sporting the biggest grin she'd ever seen on him. He then helped her carry her things back to their place. He'd cleaned off the desk and made sure there was no grease on the seat before she settled in.

But now it was over a week later, and she was floundering. She was completely confused as to what they wanted from her. They'd said all the right things at lunch and showed her more pleasure than she'd ever imagined possible. Then every day since, they'd both kissed her often and seemed to be mentally stripping her with their hot gazes whenever they looked her way. But neither of them ever touched her or took it further.

She leaned back in the seat and crossed her arms over her chest as she glared at the men working. Even at that first lunch playtime they hadn't taken her. What kind of men didn't have sex with a willing woman? Especially if they were meant to be mates for life, or whatever the hell they were. Maybe her scars had scared them away, and they'd just brought her to climax out of pity for her? Or to keep her distracted from questioning them further.

Kane twisted to face her, and his gaze caught hers. She frowned when she saw what looked like shock followed by anger flare briefly in his irises before he turned away. That damn lump in her throat returned, making it difficult to breathe as he spoke to Jeremy and snatched up a rag to wipe his hands.

Abigail rubbed her chest over her aching heart. Maybe she should go back to university. Get away from Walawuru and all this shifter stuff. She'd dye her hair and forget all about what she could be. Eventually, she'd try to find a normal man who wouldn't cringe at her scars. Not that the twins had done that exactly. A shiver ran over her at the memory of how they'd kissed and caressed the marks. Surely, they wouldn't have done that if they didn't care?

"Baby, don't cry."

With a quick breath, Abigail jerked in her seat as Jeremy turned it toward where he was kneeling. With gentle thumbs, he wiped away the tears she'd been unaware of. Blinking her eyes clear, she looked closely at his face. He seemed genuinely concerned.

"Tell me what's wrong."

She'd been trying to work out how to ask them for days, but still couldn't find the right words, so she just blurted it out and hoped it made sense, "Why did neither of you have sex with me? Why have you both not touched me since our first lunch together? Is it the scars? Were you pretending at lunch?"

Can you not stand the sight of me now? She couldn't voice that last part, but it rang loud in her mind. She shifted her gaze to the ground, unable to look at their handsome faces. Kane's knees came into view when he lowered himself beside his twin before he took her hand between his.

"You think we don't want you?"

"What else am I supposed to think?"

She hated that her voice cracked, and she cleared her throat in an attempt to cover it.

"Honey, neither of us has ever wanted a woman as much as we want you. Hell, we both came in our pants like bloody teenagers when we had you naked and between us! Surely, that should have given you at least a hint as to how much we both want you."

"But you didn't try to take me. Either of you."

"If we'd made love to you, baby, we would have bonded you to us. We wanted to wait until you felt stronger after your attack before we asked you for that honour. We need *you* to be sure that you want *us* for the rest of your life before we bond. There's no going back, Abigail."

She jerked her head up and frowned at Jeremy. "That's the only reason you haven't put the moves on me?"

Jeremy leaned in, cupped her face in his palms, and took possession of her mouth. Her mind stopped racing with questions, and she groaned at how wonderful it was to have him possess her like this. Dancing his tongue with hers, he caused her mind to fog before he pulled back, leaving her sitting in a daze, unable to move or think.

"That and we've both been working our asses off to get all the jobs done so we can take a couple days off with you this weekend."

The fog cleared and she frowned. "This weekend?"

A shudder ran through her when Kane gently bit her lower ear before he whispered into it, "Want to come camping with us for the weekend?"

They wanted to go camping?

"Seriously? Camping?"

Jeremy kissed his way along her jaw and up to her other ear. "This will be a camping trip you'll never forget. I promise. There'll be a full moon high in the sky, and the three of us beneath it, bonding."

Tingles were running through her body at their attention, and those butterflies in her belly were going berserk. They were both laying small kisses over her face, neck, and shoulders.

"So, you're asking me to bond with you?" Her voice was breathy and sounded sultry even to her own ears.

"Precisely, baby. We want you to be ours forever."

Elation and relief flowed over her and made her tremble from head to foot. They weren't rejecting her.

"Yes. Of course, yes."

Both Jeremy and Kane sat back from her and threw their heads back with hoots of joy. With a wide grin pulling at her cheeks, she knew she'd made the right decision. That these two men would always take good care of her.

six

Hammering the last of the pegs in, Jeremy stood and stretched out his back. The tent was all ready to go. He hoped Kane was done with the inside. Walking around to the front to check on his twin, he shook his head with a chuckle. Abigail was sitting on the tailgate of their ute with Kane between her thighs, kissing the hell out of her. His twin was so easily sidetracked.

"Oi, Kane! Did you get the mattress inside before our sweet, little Abigail distracted you?"

His twin pulled back from their mate. "Do you see a bed lying around out here? Of course, I got it all set up."

Jeremy peeked inside and sure enough, the big mattress was spread out with several blankets tossed on and around it. He grinned. Apparently, "make the bed" meant different things to each of them. Not that Jeremy could blame Kane. He couldn't wait to make Abigail theirs either. Giving her time to make sure she knew what she was agreeing to had been hell.

He headed in and neatened up the tent. They'd forgone an air mattress for a real one. Having three people on a blow-up would be like trying to sleep on a trampoline, especially since they had no intention of leaving her alone all weekend. One of the many reasons he loved having a ute—so simple to just toss whatever you needed in the back before driving off.

He wiped his damp palms down his thighs as he headed back out and looked to the west at the sun that was nearly down past the horizon. Sunsets and sunrises were epic in the outback. No pollution to mar their beauty, every single one was spectacular. He turned to face Abigail. Of course, his mate was so much prettier than any sunset. Moving over to stand next to Kane, who was kissing his way down her throat, Jeremy took her lips with his then moaned in bliss at her sweet taste. He would never tire of it.

"You ready, baby?" He pulled away enough to take in her expression. She looked a little scared, but mostly excited, and definitely aroused. He could smell her tangy musk floating in the air around them.

"I'm ready."

With his blood sizzling with a mix of anticipation and excitement, he pulled his shirt over his head and tossed it in the bed of the ute behind her. Kane had her shirt unbuttoned already, so he helped his twin remove it along with her bra. Her nipples tightened instantly when they were hit with the cool evening air.

"So beautiful."

He bent down to suckle one into his mouth. Her hand came up and held his head to her as she arched into the contact. He released her flesh reluctantly and stood to see Kane had her shoes off and had begun to strip himself. Jeremy toed off his boots and shucked his pants and boxers, so he stood before his mate stark naked. Her gaze flicked between him and Kane, the tip of her tongue coming out to lick her lips. He lowered his hand to stroke himself a couple of times. Even with a tight fist, it did nothing to ease the ache. The damn thing had a mind of its own, and it knew full well Abigail was sitting in front of him. No way was it going to settle for a hand job today.

"Scoot forward, honey."

He gave himself one last stroke while Kane

helped her off the tailgate and moved in to take her mouth with his. She wound her hands around his twin's neck and closed her eyes. Jeremy moved up to stand behind her as Kane reached between them and undid her jeans. He pushed them, along with her knickers, down over her hips. Jeremy took them from there, lifting her feet one at a time to free her of the material. On his way up, he pressed kisses and took nips of the flesh up the backs of her thighs and ass. He licked up her spine, loving the way she shivered beneath him as his head buzzed from her flavour.

Kane released her mouth, and Jeremy ran his palms down her arms until he covered her hands. Tangling their fingers together, he pulled her hands up behind his neck.

"Keep them there, baby."

His skin lit up with how good it felt to have her soft fingers wrapped around the back of his neck. He trailed his palms down until they covered her high breasts.

"Aren't we going to lie down in the tent?"

Her husky voice brought out every one of his instincts.

"Not this first time, baby. This first time when we join and bond, we'll be standing beneath the moon. Then we'll fly free together."

"Oh."

He tugged on her hard nipples, earning himself a moan from her sweet mouth. Kane lifted one of her legs and held it over his hip as his other hand went to her core. He felt her body tighten when his twin began stroking her.

"She's so wet already, Jer. You want this as badly as we do, don't you, honey?"

"Uh huh."

She was grinding her hips against Kane's hand, and Jeremy couldn't help but thrust his erection against her ass as she did. He couldn't wait to be inside her. To join with her at the same time Kane did. Finally, they were going to bond with their mate, claim her forever, and his blood sang with elation. He turned his head to lay kisses over her upper arm and shoulder, barely noticing the scars beneath his lips until he could whisper in her ear.

"I love you, Abigail. I'm going to always protect you and keep you safe."

Kane leaned in and kissed her mouth again. He couldn't stop. Didn't want to. He was completely addicted, and totally happy about it.

"Same here, honey. I love you and vow to always keep you safe."

With one hand still holding her thigh over his hip, he grabbed his aching erection with the other and lined it up with her slick heat. A moan tore from his throat as he pressed the head of his dick into her tight channel. Before he went deeper, he shifted his hand to move her other leg to wrap around him. She was now totally reliant on them to hold her up and not let her fall. The show of her trust in them was a total turn-on and had Kane wanting nothing more than to impale her quickly over his dick. But he had to be careful with her this first time, ease her into accepting his presence within her.

She didn't protest at all as he sank slowly deeper, but rather arched into him, taking more of him inside her body. He shifted his hands to her hips and buried himself to the hilt within her. Her soft, wet heat surrounded him, and the sensation left his head spinning. His blood sizzled in his veins as he gave her a few slow thrusts before he held still, fully seated within her.

"Lean on me, honey. Wrap your arms around my neck."

Jeremy helped guide her until she pressed against him. A grunt escaped him when her rock-hard little nipples poked at his chest. Her head dropped into the crook of his neck, and he shuddered when her hot lips and tongue stroked against his sweat-slicked skin. She clenched her inner muscles around him, and he groaned aloud. He'd never last if she kept that up.

"Jer, you gotta hurry, man. She's gripping me like a vise. I'm not sure how long I can last."

When the pop of a bottle opening sounded, Abigail's body tensed up.

"Shhh, Abigail. Jeremy's going to get you ready to take us both. It won't hurt if we do it right. Just relax against me and let him do his thing with that sweet little ass of yours."

Her arms tightened around his neck and she whimpered, but after a few seconds, she started flexing her hips back and forth between them. Her grip loosened and he couldn't keep still any longer. He started pumping into her with a slow, lazy rhythm that would keep her on edge and enjoying what they were doing to her.

"Hurry up, Jer. I can't resist her much longer."

"She's ready. Let me lube up."

"You may as well speak out loud. I can hear you either way."

"Cheeky girl, how long have you been able to hear us?"

Kane gritted his teeth when she chuckled and her whole body vibrated against his.

"You'll never know."

"Minx."

Jeremy bit her shoulder, and she shuddered again.

"Jer, stop making her clench!"

The bastard grinned and winked at him before he finally moved up close behind her and started pressing into her. Abigail gasped and tightened her grip once more. He shuddered when her fingernails dug into the flesh of his shoulders. He loved that she'd marked him with her passion.

"Deep breaths and push back against him, honey. Just like you did with his fingers."

She panted and groaned but followed his instructions and pushed her ass back toward his twin. Jeremy slid home and her channel squeezed around his erection.

"Bloody hell, you are so fucking tight, honey."

Jeremy made a rumble in agreement before

he pulled back. When his twin thrust back in, Kane pulled out and they set a fast, hard rhythm. Not wanting to take any chance she'd fall from them, he kept his fingers wrapped around her thighs, holding her securely as their sweaty skin allowed them to slide easily against each other.

After a minute or so, she released her death grip on him, and he relished the sting where she'd pierced his flesh with her nails. Her sweaty skin gleamed in the moonlight as she arched her spine and leaned back against Jeremy. His brother instantly covered her perky little breasts with his hands, tugging and pulling at her stiff nipples until she was whimpering and writhing between them.

She had one hand on his shoulder and the other tangled in Jeremy's hair. Her body was flushed with her arousal, and the moonlight made her look like a goddess. Which was appropriate—she was one. She was their goddess and always would be.

With his firm grip on her, he easily slid her back and forth between him and his twin, loving the feel of her soft, wet heat against his erection as he moved her. He sucked in a breath when she dug her heels into his ass a moment before her channel tightened around him. She was getting close, which was a good thing because he wasn't far behind her.

"That's it, honey, you're nearly there, aren't you?"

They all needed to climax together to cement the bond between them. Then the magic would kick in and things would get really interesting. He'd only heard stories about what happened when a trio bonded. His body tightened and his erection jerked within her as he closed in on his orgasm. He couldn't wait to be fully bonded with his mate, his sweet little Abigail. She was everything he could have dreamed of for a mate. She was strong—a survivor—but still had her kind heart and sweet personality. Unable to resist, he leaned in and took her mouth in a searing kiss before he jerked back and looked around him at the red sparks filling the air.

"Abigail, honey, open your eyes. You don't want to miss this."

Her body hummed with arousal. She was sure she could actually feel her blood sizzle in her veins, she was that hot. She forced her lids open and gasped at the red sparks floating around them. A groan ripped from her as Jeremy slid a hand down from her breast to press against her clit as he thrust in at the same time as Kane. They'd been taking turns, and she'd loved how it had felt sliding between her two men, but now they were both fully impaled inside her, and she felt their erections kick and jerk as they reached for their climaxes.

"Come, baby. Now!"

Jeremy continued to rub her clit and they both thrust into her again, and that was it. She threw her head back, thumping it against Jeremy's chest as she tightened her grip on Kane's shoulder and Jeremy's neck. The orgasm was so intense, her mind blacked out for a moment. She came back to herself, panting for breath and feeling like her entire being was vibrating. The men slipped from her body, and Jeremy's hands moved to cup her bottom as Kane kept a tight hold on her thighs.

"You ready to fly, honey?"

What? She'd already flown. She wasn't entirely sure all her pieces had returned yet from how hard she'd shattered just now. With a frown, she faced Kane, about to ask what he was on about when her body jerked. She tensed up as a wave of heat flowed over her, leaving her skin feeling tight, like she'd grown bigger within it. As she gulped in a breath of air, she saw more red sparks. So many, her vision turned a glittery red. Her mind whirled with panic, and she screamed when the men threw her high in the air. She hadn't anticipated it, and she certainly hadn't expected to flash into a Wedge-tailed eagle as she flew up through the night sky.

Her heart raced in her chest, and she instinctively spread her wings and flapped them. Bloody hell! She was flying! Like, really flying. She was a freaking eagle! She laughed, but it came out as a noise so horrid, she stopped immediately. *Okay, mental note. I can't speak as a bird.*

"You can speak, baby. It's just different, and you can always reach us telepathically."

She glanced to either side of her and watched Jeremy and Kane effortlessly flying alongside her while she jerked up and down, still trying to get the hang of using her wings.

"Can you show me how to do this right?"

"Of course, baby."

Twenty minutes later, they flew back to their campsite. Abigail couldn't remember ever feeling freer or happier. She loved flying, the feel of the wind in her feathers as she'd circled in a thermal to get high above the earth with her males on either side making sure she was safe.

Focusing on the sand near the rear of the ute, she used her wings like the men had told her to slow her descent until her feet touched the ground. She had to run a few steps and nearly tumbled into a heap, but she caught herself in time to prevent some serious embarrassment. She watched in awe as both men landed gracefully in front of her.

"Wish I looked that good landing."

"You will soon enough. Like anything, it takes a little practice."

"Okay, how do I be human again?"

"Close your eyes and focus on calling to your human side. Let it flow through you, and you'll shift."

She closed her eyes and followed Jeremy's instructions. A flash of heat passed through her, and on a gasp, her eyes flew open, and she stood before them naked. She wriggled her toes and fingers and rolled her shoulders to make sure everything worked before she looked up at her men with joy filling her. They both stood in all their naked human glory before her with wide grins and hard bodies. Nothing hurt now. Her leg had started to ache earlier, but was fine now, and her burn scars didn't pull or itch. She still had the marks, but everything underneath was now healed. Elation filled her and she threw herself at them, knowing with one hundred percent surety that they'd catch her. She was still struggling with how she'd managed to land two such marvellous males as her lifelong mates, but right now it didn't matter how or why. The only thing that really mattered was that they were both all hers. Laughing, she landed against them, and they wrapped her up in their arms.

"I love you both so much. Thank you for everything you've done for me, and for putting up with my stupid insecurities."

"They weren't stupid, baby. You had every right to question what was happening between us and why. Just know that now we're bonded for life, nothing will ever separate us or come between us. We're a fully bonded family unit."

Her lower belly tightened with arousal at being touched by them both. She slid a hand up each of their necks, tangling her fingers in their hair before she pulled first Kane down for a quick kiss, then Jeremy for his.

"So, you two set that tent up for a reason or what?"

"Minx."

She squealed with delight as Kane slung

her over his shoulder and headed into the tent, where he tossed her onto the mattress. She lay there squirming and giggling as her men both stood there stroking their hard erections and looking at every inch of her body. Then, they moved to lay on either side of her and each pressed one hand over her flat belly.

"You know, honey, in our family, every female has fallen pregnant on their bonding night."

"Is that so?" The very thought of having their baby had her heart filling with joy, and she couldn't wait for it to happen. "Guess we should give it our best shot then. I mean, who are we to mess with tradition?"

They both fell on her, smothering her with kisses and caresses until she couldn't think anymore. Yes, this was going to be a great weekend. The first of many, she was sure.

Thank you so much for reading Scarred Perfection. I hope you enjoyed reading Jeremy, Kane and Abigail's story as much as I did writing it. Please consider leaving a review.

Want to know about new releases and what events I'll be at? Get a free ebook?
Sign up for my author newsletter at
www.khloewren.com

biography

Khloe Wren lives in rural South Australia with her husband, two daughters and an ever changing list of animals!

She started writing in 2013 and has published over 50 books since then in the romantic suspense genre. She writes both paranormal and contemporary stories, including her best selling series Charon MC.

Khloe enjoys writing outside of the box and she loves her heroes strong, and her heroines even stronger.

facebook.com/khloe.wren.3

instagram.com/khloewren

bookbub.com/authors/khloewren

acknowledgments

I wrote this story back in 2015. This was an incredibly hard year for me as I had a particularly nasty bout of depression take me down. I wrote this story after a family trip up through the centre of South Australia. We stopped at a small town on the main highway heading up through the Flinders Ranges, this town only had a handful of buildings on the main highway, and one of those included the cutest little roadhouse that had been an old homestead in a previous life. The older couple running it were lovely, but sadly I didn't write their names down and can no longer remember.

That trip certainly had some highs and lows, and included a fun afternoon drive where we went bush (off any roads and just went exploring) and didn't realise that no one had remembered to pack water. Our old car over heated and man, I've honestly never been so worried we weren't going to make it as I was that day! When we finally got to a main road, I think all of us wanted to get out and kiss that bitumen that meant we could now find a town.

This story was first published with a small press, and I got the rights back this year so I've edited over it, modernised a few things, and now republishing it.

This story has always been one of my favourite stories. While I don't have the outer scars like Abigail, but my insides are scarred as hell, and I have the most wonderful husband who indeed loves all my scarred perfection no matter how bad it gets.

So this book is dedicated to Steve, the best, most patient and loving man I could have ever hoped to find, or be blessed to be married to. Love you, babe!

Xo
Khloe